TOB

D0533821

Can an old toy pan~~~ ~~~ ~~~ children stand up to their bullying minder?

Jenny Nimmo worked at the BBC for a number of years, ending in a spell as a director/adaptor for *Jackanory*. Her book *The Snow Spider* won the 1986 Smarties Book Prize and, with the other two books in the trilogy, *Emlyn's Moon* and *The Chestnut Soldier*, was made into a popular television series. Among her other titles are *The Owl-tree*, Winner of a Smarties Prize Gold Award (6–8 Category), *Dog Star, Ronnie and the Giant Millipede* and *The Stone Mouse*, which was shortlisted for the Carnegie Medal. Jenny Nimmo lives in a converted watermill in Wales with her artist husband and three children.

Helen Craig has illustrated many children's books, including *The Town Mouse and the Country Mouse* (shortlisted for the 1992 Smarties Book Prize), four *This Is the Bear* books and *The Stone Mouse*.

It was dark in the attic and Toby wondered if he was really awake or still dreaming.

Toby in the Dark

Written by
JENNY NIMMO

Illustrated by
HELEN CRAIG

WALKER BOOKS
AND SUBSIDIARIES
LONDON • BOSTON • SYDNEY

First published 1999 by Walker Books Ltd
87 Vauxhall Walk, London SE11 5HJ

This edition published 1999

2 4 6 8 10 9 7 5 3

Text © 1999 Jenny Nimmo
Illustrations © 1999 Helen Craig

The right of Jenny Nimmo to be identified as author of
this work has been asserted by her in accordance with the
Copyright, Designs and Patents Act 1988.

This book has been typeset in Plantin Light.

Printed by J.H. Haynes & Co Ltd, Sparkford

British Library Cataloguing in Publication Data
A catalogue record for this book is
available from the British Library.

ISBN 0-7445-6976-1

For Luke and Max
J.N.

For Marissa, Eva and Jonathan
with love
H.C.

CONTENTS

When Mrs Malevant stepped through the Smiths' front door, the hall suddenly seemed to get darker.

CHAPTER ONE

When Mrs Malevant stepped through the Smiths' front door, the hall suddenly seemed to get darker.

"I'm used to children," said the new minder. "I even know what they're up to when no one's looking. So don't, for one moment, think you can get away with anything wicked." She was tall and broad with a voice like a rusty saw.

The four Smith children backed away, even Sam, who was big for twelve and thought himself tough. Miranda, two years younger, hid behind him. Bert hid behind Izzy.

Mrs Malevant had come to take care of

them while their parents were away, visiting Gran and Grandpa in Australia. A kind, motherly person had been expected. Someone who liked children. Mrs Malevant clearly did not.

The children weren't quite sure what to do next, so they showed the new minder into the kitchen. And then wished they hadn't. She frowned at the pile of saucepans and the dirty plates in the sink. She glared at the crumbs on the floor and the mess on the table. And Izzy noticed shadows deepening in corners and a chilly draught spring up from nowhere.

"Well, introduce yourselves," Mrs Malevant commanded, plonking her suitcase down. The house gave a little groan, and one of Bert's marbles – a marble that had been sitting perfectly still for almost a week – suddenly rolled out from under the dresser.

"I'm Sam," said Sam.

"Samuel," the minder corrected him. "I don't like abbreviations."

"Miranda," said Miranda.

"Nice name." Mrs Malevant nodded approvingly.

"Izzy," said Izzy. "What are abbreviations?"

Mrs Malevant gave Izzy a long, hard look. "Shortenings," she said. "Slang. Laziness. Your name, for instance, is Isabella. I've heard all about you, Isabella. Eight years old and not to be trusted."

Izzy, who was always friendly, felt her smile slide into her boots. "Me?" she said. "Who told you that? Not Mum, I bet."

Mrs Malevant ignored her. "As for you, Herbert," she spoke to the only part of Bert she could see, his feet. "It's time you stopped hiding behind things. Let me have a look at you."

Bert stayed where he was. Behind Izzy.

"Bert's shy," said Izzy. "Leave him alone till he's ready."

"Hold your tongue," said Mrs Malevant. "Herbert, come here."

At that moment the house gave a shudder and there was a loud thump from above. Everyone glanced upwards. The sound seemed to come from the attic.

"What's that?" Mrs Malevant looked directly at Izzy, as though Izzy were responsible.

Izzy shrugged. "Maybe our auntie fell over," she said.

"You mean your great-aunt," said Mrs Malevant. "Where's her room?"

"Next floor up," Sam told her. "That's where you'll be sleeping. Adults on the middle floor. Children at the top."

"I'm going to have my work cut out, I can

*The house gave a shudder and there was a loud thump
from above. Everyone glanced upwards.*

see," snorted the minder. "Four trouble-some children and two old folk to manage."

"Great-uncle Maurice won't be any trouble," Miranda promised. "You'll hardly notice him. He lives in a world of his own."

"A world of his own," whispered Bert as Aunt Folly came bundling in.

"I'm so glad you've come," Aunt Folly said to the minder. "My brother, Maurice, and I meant to have a nice tea waiting for you, but well ... I just can't seem to manage." She held out a hand. "How do you do, Mrs Malevant. I'm Miss Smith, but do call me Folly."

Mrs Malevant frowned at Aunt Folly, who wore several necklaces, a long flowery skirt and loads of lipstick, badly applied.

"How d'you do, Miss Smith," she said. "I prefer to be formal."

When the two women shook hands there was a sudden, really loud rumble from the

14

attic, as though a pile of cases had toppled over.

"Is your house falling down?" asked Mrs Malevant.

"No, no," said Aunt Folly. "But it's an old house. It *feels* things. I know this sounds silly, but sometimes it gets a bit … troubled, if you know what I mean."

"I don't think I do," said the minder.

Izzy had the strangest feeling that something had woken up, something that had been asleep for a long, long time.

The suitcase had fallen from the top of a pile,
and the panda had tumbled out.

CHAPTER TWO

Izzy was right. Something in the attic had woken up: an old toy panda.

His name was Toby and he'd been asleep for sixty-five years, packed tight in a suitcase whose locks had sprung open when the old house shuddered. The suitcase had fallen from the top of a pile, and the panda had tumbled out.

It was dark in the attic and Toby wondered if he was really awake or still dreaming. His eyes didn't seem to be working as well as they should. Who was he? Where were his friends? And then he remembered Boy. He would call to Boy and Boy would come and find him. How had they ever become parted? The panda had forgotten.

Toby got to his feet, rather shakily. All he could see was a cobwebby jungle of cases and furniture. Wherever he was, there seemed to be no way out.

"Boy!" he called. "Help me!"

No reply. Toby shivered. Something was wrong. The house wasn't happy. That's why it had woken him up. "Boy!" he called again. "Help me!" Again no reply. It was all too much for a panda on his first day awake after sixty-five years. So he curled up in the dust and cobwebs and fell fast asleep again.

But not for long this time. Next morning the sound of voices woke him up. The panda rolled over and discovered that he was lying beside a trapdoor. He put out a paw and found a small gap between the floor and the door. Wide enough for a panda? He peeped down into the passage below; he could hear footsteps, running water, banging doors. If he wriggled closer he could… "Ooooo," he squeaked. "Now I've done it!"

Toby was falling into the strange, half-forgotten world of bright colours and children's voices. He landed right at Bert's feet.

"Something fell through the ceiling," cried Bert. "Look, everyone!"

"Don't touch it!" Miranda sidled out of her room. "It's come from the attic. Look, the trapdoor's open. That thing might've been run over by rats."

Bert didn't notice the panda shudder. "D'you mean run over, like by a car?" he asked. "Rats aren't very heavy."

"No, Bert." Miranda sighed. Seen from Toby's point of view she was very tall with long pale legs and yellow hair.

Another boy appeared. He was even taller than Miranda and his hair had been cut so short it was hardly there at all. "What Miranda really means," he said, "is that the thing," a toe touched Toby, "might've been peed on by rats."

"What is it? What is it?" another voice sang out. "Let me see." A head poked its way between Miranda and Sam, a head of dark untidy curls.

"It's a sort of bear, I think," said Sam.

"It's a panda," Izzy declared. "I didn't know there was a panda in the house!"

At last, someone who knows, thought the panda.

Izzy knelt and reached out a hand towards Toby, while Miranda warned, "Be careful, it's dirty."

"Then I'll clean him up," said Izzy.

She took the panda into her room and laid

"It's a panda," Izzy declared. *"I didn't know there was a panda in the house!"*

him on the bed. "Now let's have a look at you." She studied the panda for a moment, seeing a small bear-shaped creature with worn and patchy fur. His arms, legs, ears and chest were black, while his bottom half and his face were white. Definitely a panda, but there was something missing.

"Your eyes," Izzy exclaimed. "What happened to them?"

In place of the shiny black beads that would have given the panda a wholesome look, someone had stitched two scraps of grey cloth.

So there is something wrong, thought Toby. *I knew it. My eyesight used to be perfect.*

Using her hairbrush, Izzy began to pull the dust and cobwebs off him. The brush was rather spiky but it was nice getting so much attention after all the years of neglect, so the panda didn't complain.

"Where's Boy?" he asked.

But Izzy did not reply. She kept right on brushing. She began to hum as she worked, turning the panda over and over, upside down, back to front, into his ears and over his nose. On every finger she wore a ring and their sparkle dazzled the panda.

"I know Boy is here – somewhere," Toby said, as though he were having a conversation and not being held upside down, "because I can feel it. I think he might need me, that's why I woke up."

"Isabella, are you ready? You've got five minutes for breakfast." A distant and rather bad-tempered voice reached Izzy and the panda.

"Oops!" squealed Izzy. "Got to go now, Panda. School. I'll see you later." Dropping him on to her bed, she flew off, grabbing bags and books as she went.

"Just tell me where..." began Toby. And then he realized: *She can't hear me. No one can hear me!* It had taken him ages to get through to Boy. To teach him how to stay really, really still and listen. Now he would have to start all over again with this girl.

He sat up and looked round the room. Even with his poor eyesight he could see that it was very untidy; drawers coughing up clothes, pencils, paper; books and toys everywhere, even a dog. A *dog*? Oh, a stuffed dog, asleep. Nothing to worry about.

Toby slipped off the bed and ran into the passage. One end was dark, the other lit by a large window. The panda moved towards the light. The staircase took him by surprise. He stumbled down the first step, then rolled all the way down to the next landing, where he lay very still, half the life knocked out of him.

After a while the panda sensed a movement, quite close. A door opening. Footsteps.

"Boy," sighed Toby. "At last."

Boy stood beside him, a looming, bulky shape. The panda searched for Boy's face, far above. Something had happened to Boy – he was different. But still Boy.

"It's me," Toby whispered. "You know, *me*!"

He waited, hopefully, while Boy stood motionless, gazing at his feet. Then Boy thrust his hands into his pockets and walked down the stairs.

The panda couldn't believe it. "Don't you know who I am?" he called. "Boy, what's happened to you?"

"Where's the panda that was on my bed?"
Izzy asked Mrs Malevant.

Chapter Three

Izzy's day had been very bad. She'd forgotten to do her homework and all her rings had been confiscated. She wasn't supposed to wear jewellery in school, but it made her feel closer to Mum. When Mum dressed up she looked fantastic with her silver necklace and big silver rings. Izzy didn't feel safe without Mum, but now, at least, there was Panda waiting at home for her.

When Izzy got home and found the panda had gone from her room, she ran down to the kitchen. "Where's the panda that was on my bed?" she asked Mrs Malevant.

"What panda?" Mrs Malevant squinted at Izzy through a cloud of steam.

"You know what panda," said Izzy, with a sigh of impatience.

"I do not. You are a rude child, Isabella Smith. The rudest I've met. And one day you'll get your comeuppance." Mrs Malevant turned her attention to the commotion on the stove.

"And you'll get yours," murmured Izzy. "I want my mum."

"Well, you're not going to get her," said Mrs Malevant. "Not for two whole weeks. And I wouldn't blame her if she never came back with a child like you at the end of her journey. Now sit down and eat your nice tea."

Izzy was speechless. She took her place at the kitchen table while the others filed into the room.

Mrs Malevant handed out plates of brown food. It didn't look nice at all.

"What is it?" asked Sam.

"Food," said the minder. "Now, eat it!"

Izzy wondered how long they would last, eating such horrible food. Upstairs there was an old lady who could have cooked their teas, and even done the washing. (There was an old man too, but he hardly counted.) Aunt Folly said she couldn't cope, so Mum had hired Mrs Malevant, but Izzy believed Aunt Folly could have coped perfectly well. She was just scared of trying.

When the children had finished their tea, they stacked the plates in the dishwasher that Dad had bought especially for the minder's convenience. Then they crept away in a bunch, sticking close together until they were out of her range.

*   *   *

29

At the bottom of the wash-basket, the panda lay badly squashed but wide awake. Mrs Malevant had scooped him off the stairs and chucked him in the basket on her way to gather dirty clothes. He couldn't see anything but he had heard enough to realize that this was a very unhappy house. Mrs Malevant would have to go.

Stuffed toys don't move when they're being watched, except in emergencies. This was an emergency. For Izzy's sake Toby would have to scare Mrs Malevant away. Nothing else would shift her. He began a long struggle with the dirty clothes on top of him.

Mrs Malevant grunted and puffed as she scrubbed burnt remains from the saucepans. She didn't notice the shuffling and heaving in the basket until the panda had almost reached the top. Then a slight rustle alerted her. She stared suspiciously into the corner.

Toby, aware of the sudden silence, knew that he had her attention. Concentrating all his strength in his small feet, he paddled against a pair of jeans for a moment, then launched himself upwards. He shot past a wet towel, flew into the air, and fell back into the basket.

Mrs Malevant had a magnificent scream. It could have been used in horror movies. "Eeeeeee-ooooooo-owwwwwww!"

Aunt Folly ran into the kitchen crying, "What's happened, Mrs M? Are you hurt?"

"That thing moved!" Mrs Malevant pointed at the panda. "It jumped right out of the basket. And don't call me Mrs M."

"Oh, I'm sorry." Aunt Folly blushed and looked in the basket. "What a dirty little toy, and yet I seem to..." She turned to Mrs

Malevant. "Sit down, dear. What you need is a strong cup of tea."

"It's that girl," grumbled Mrs Malevant. "Isabella. She's wicked. Plays tricks. She should be punished."

"She misses her mother," said Aunt Folly. "Children aren't wicked."

"Oh, ho. Aren't they?" Mrs Malevant muttered crustily.

"I never had children," said Aunt Folly, busying herself with the teapot and kettle, "but I've lived here with these four since they were born. They've made it such a happy house." She gave an anxious glance at the ceiling. "At least until recently."

A silence fell.

Toby waited for Aunt Folly to speak again. Her voice was familiar. If only she would say a bit more, he might guess who she was.

Then someone else came into the kitchen.

Heavy footsteps. Slow and rather uncertain.

"Hullo, dear, I've just made some tea," said Aunt Folly. "Poor Mrs Malevant's had a bit of a turn."

"Not a *turn*," Mrs Malevant protested. "A scare. Someone played a trick on me. That dirty toy in the wash-basket jumped right into the air. I'll throw it in the fire. That'll teach them."

The panda gasped. A shadow fell over the basket and someone looked down on him. "Boy," he said happily.

Uncle Maurice stared at Toby for a long time, and then he walked away.

"Boy!" called Toby. "Don't let her burn me!"

Bert shuffled back to the door, glancing at the basket of washing as he passed.

CHAPTER FOUR

I must get away, thought the panda. He tried to move again but his leap from the basket had exhausted him. Besides, he had already broken the rules once today. He would have to gather his strength and wait until dark. But suppose Mrs Malevant decided to burn him before he could make his escape?

"Can I have a cookie?" Bert had come back to the kitchen. "A chocolate one?"

"You cannot," said Mrs Malevant. "You've had your tea."

"Just one," he pleaded.

"It wouldn't hurt," said Aunt Folly. "Would it, Mrs Malevant?"

"Rules are rules," she snapped.

"You'd better run along then, Bert," Aunt Folly said sadly.

Bert shuffled back to the door, glancing at the basket of washing as he passed.

"Pick me up!" said the panda.

Bert stopped and looked down at Toby. He opened his mouth to speak but something told him not to. While Mrs Malevant had her back to him he bent down quickly, scooped up the panda and hid him under his sweater. As soon as he left the kitchen, Bert ran very fast, up two flights of stairs, along a corridor and into Izzy's room. "Look!" he cried. "The panda!"

"Bert, you're brilliant!" Izzy took the panda and hugged him. "Where was he?"

"In with the washing."

Izzy gasped. "She'd have put him in the machine. He might've drowned."

"I nearly missed him," Bert said. "But then I … well, it was like he spoke to me, although he didn't even open his mouth or anything."

"Hmm." Izzy looked thoughtful. "I'd better keep him hidden. Mrs Malevant might do something worse next time she finds him. Thanks, Bert. I owe you a favour."

"I could do with a cookie," said Bert. "A chocolate one."

"I'll get some for you when Mrs M's not in the kitchen. Promise."

"Thanks." Bert's sad face lit up. He ran off and Izzy began to wonder how she could keep her promise.

"I've noticed that Mrs M locks the kitchen cupboard," she told the panda, never dreaming that he understood. "So none of us can have cookies or crisps or chocolate when we want. Nothing that would make us happy."

"That's bad," said the panda.

Izzy still didn't hear him. "I'll just have to get the key somehow," she went on. "I bet she keeps it in her room. Maybe on the dressing-table, or by her bed."

Izzy sat still for a long time, holding the panda tight while the house got darker. Dark and sad. All the good things seemed to have vanished: the treats and comforts and good-night kisses. All gone. Nothing left but shadowy corners and Mrs Malevant.

All at once, Izzy felt very tired. She got into bed and fell fast asleep, only to wake with a strange whispering in her ear.

"Izzy! Izzy!"

Izzy sat up. In the pale starlight that filled her room she could just make out the panda lying on her pillow.

Izzy got into bed and fell fast asleep, only to wake with a strange whispering in her ear.

"Did you … speak?" she asked nervously.

"Yes," said Toby. "I'm glad you heard me. I was beginning to think I'd lost my voice."

Izzy stared at the panda, and then she asked, "Can you move as well?"

"Not while I'm being watched. Not as a rule."

"What's your name?"

"I've forgotten it," said the panda.

"Then I shall call you Panda until you remember." Izzy gave him a sudden hug. "I'm so glad I found you," she said. "Life's been horrible lately." And she told the panda all about the good times that had vanished when Mum and Dad went to Australia.

She told him about her family, and how the first letters of all their names spelled Smith, which made them a very special family. "Samuel, Miranda, Izzy and Herbert," she said. "Only Herbert prefers to be called Bert."

"S-M-I-H," murmured the panda. "So whose name begins with T?"

"That was for Thomas the cat, only he got run over," said Izzy. She sighed. "Perhaps that's when our troubles began. We're not a whole family now."

"What about Boy?" asked the panda.

"D'you mean Bert or Sam?"

"Not Bert. Not Sam," said the panda. "Another boy. He's here. I know it. I've seen him."

"Then he must be a ghost," said Izzy.

Luckily the door was open, just a fraction. Toby tugged it wide enough to let himself through.

CHAPTER FIVE

Toby was lost for words. Boy, a *ghost*? How was it possible? "He's not a ghost, he's a person," the panda told Izzy. But Izzy had fallen asleep.

"Now's the time to get the cookies," said Toby. "Shall I find the key for you?"

There was no reply, so Toby slid off the bed and marched to the door. Luckily this was open, just a fraction. He tugged it wide enough to let himself through.

The passage outside was pitch dark but the panda wasn't deterred. He made his way down to the next landing. Mrs Malevant slept in the first room he came to; he could hear her snoring through the half-open door. Toby slipped into the room and jumped on to a stool by the dressing-table.

A big bunch of keys lay within easy reach. Toby slid the key-ring over his paw and ran out. The rest was easy. Unobserved, the panda could move like lightning. In no time at all he'd unlocked the kitchen cupboard, seized the tin of cookies and replaced the keys on Mrs Malevant's dressing-table.

Bert's door was shut, so Toby tapped softly and dropped the tin outside. Then, feeling very pleased with himself, he made his way back to Izzy's bed and fell asleep beside her.

Bert didn't hear the gentle tap. He slept on until the early morning when a rumbling tummy woke him up. He decided to creep down to the kitchen for a piece of bread. When he opened his bedroom door he almost stepped on the cookie tin.

"Wow!" said Bert. "Cookies. Thanks, Izzy." He grabbed the cookie tin and ran back to bed. After eating four cookies he felt much better and dropped off to sleep, still nibbling.

Later that morning Bert's pillow was covered in big splotches of chocolate.

"Dirty boy!" Mrs Malevant's roar woke Izzy with a start. "You'll scrub that pillowslip until it's clean!"

Izzy ran across to Bert's room just as Mrs Malevant came marching out. "It was you," she said. "Don't deny it. You stole those cookies to get your brother into trouble."

"That's not true!" cried Bert. "I asked her to get them."

"I *knew* it." Mrs Malevant swept past, triumphant, and thumped down the groaning staircase.

"I don't understand," said Izzy.

The panda, listening from Izzy's pillow, had heard every word. So when Izzy came storming into her room, he said, quietly, "Sorry!"

Izzy stood quite still, staring at her pillow. "Panda, did you … speak?"

"Have you forgotten?" said Toby. "We had such a good chat last night."

"I thought I was dreaming," said Izzy. "It's different in daylight."

"I've mucked things up for you," said the panda. "I didn't think you'd get the blame. *I* took the cookies."

Izzy's mouth dropped open. "How?"

"It was easy," said Toby. "But I tend to rush into things without thinking. I'll make it up to you."

"There's no need…" began Izzy, only to be cut short by a shout from below.

"Breakfast," she said. "I'd better dash or there'll be more trouble."

After breakfast Sam, Miranda and Izzy went to school. Bert had to scrub his pillowslip in the kitchen sink. In the afternoon he was shut in his room while he wrote a hundred lines. Or tried to. "I must not be greedy ... I must not be greedy..." He sobbed out the words as his pen scratched over the paper.

Toby crept over to Bert's room and sat outside the door. He listened to the sobs and snuffles and wished he could do something to help. He dozed off for a moment and when he woke up he found Boy standing very close.

"Boy!" said Toby. "You've come. I knew you would."

Boy put his hand on Bert's door as though to comfort him. For a moment his eyes rested on the panda at his feet, and he gave what seemed to be a bleak sort of smile. Then he walked away.

Perhaps Boy is a ghost, thought the panda. The real Boy would never walk away from someone in trouble.

Sunshine streamed into the passage from an open door and, longing for warmth, Toby bounced closer. It was Miranda's room. The panda hopped in. Compared with Izzy's, this room was wonderfully tidy. Bed made, clothes hidden in drawers, books neatly stacked and three china ducks on the dressing-table, carefully spaced.

A bright red dressing-gown lay at the foot of the bed – a perfect cloak for a panda with thin fur. Toby tugged at the shiny cord. Somehow the dressing-gown got caught on a chair. The chair fell over, hitting the dressing-table and making it wobble. The three china ducks came tumbling down. *Clink! Clink! Clink!* A headless duck rolled towards Toby.

"Oh no!" he squeaked. "I didn't mean it. I didn't want to…" He ran out of the room, straight into the path of Aunt Folly.

Toby lay flat: a lifeless stuffed toy again.

Aunt Folly looked down. "You again," she said, and picked him up. Toby trembled. "I've seen you somewhere before. Of course," she gave a little chuckle, "I can hardly believe it after all these years."

Aunt Folly's face swam closer, so close that the panda could see all the little cracks and crannies on her skin, and something else. Glinting among the coloured stones on Aunt Folly's necklace were two black beads. Toby knew they belonged to him. He began to remember the terrible thing that had happened to him long ago!

"I shall take care of you now," said Aunt Folly. She carried the panda down to the sitting-room, and when she sat in her big armchair, she tucked him in beside her.

Toby saw a shadowy room where Boy and he had played together, dozed and talked. He knew it was the same room even though everything in it had changed.

The panda heard footsteps in the hall. Aunt Folly looked up as someone came into the room and sat down. Toby couldn't quite see who it was.

"I think we ought to do something," Aunt Folly said suddenly. "I mean about the children. The agency has sent the wrong sort of person. Mrs Malevant's a bully. The house is getting worried, haven't you noticed? No one laughs any more. We should take care of the children. We don't need a minder, but I … I can't cope alone."

No one answered. Was she talking to herself, or to a ghost?

All at once Aunt Folly picked up the panda and held him out. "Look what I've found," she said. "The panda. Do you remember?" And Toby found himself staring at Boy, who was staring right back. Or was he?

"Don't you know me?" Toby asked in a whisper.

"I can see it's no use," said Aunt Folly, pushing the panda in beside her. "Don't you remember when you were a boy? How you loved that panda. You said he could talk ... and walk."

Silence followed. A silence so still and so deep that the panda felt himself almost to be dreaming. Then the door was suddenly flung open and Mrs Malevant bellowed, "Tea's ready!"

51

The dreamlike mood was shattered. Aunt Folly jumped as though something had stung her. "Mrs Malevant," she said, "I didn't hear you."

"Did I scare you?" The minder gave a nasty smile as though she hoped she'd scared Aunt Folly.

"A little. Could you take Bert something to drink, or perhaps I…"

"That's not advisable," said Mrs Malevant. "He must learn his lesson."

"I see." Aunt Folly hung her head.

Mrs Malevant turned to go and then she seemed to change her mind. She came right over to Aunt Folly and bending very close said, "I was going to wash that panda."

"Panda?" enquired Aunt Folly.

Toby held his breath and waited for Mrs Malevant to pounce. But she didn't see him hidden in Aunt Folly's shadow.

"That dirty toy," went on the minder. "I wouldn't really have burnt it. That was just my little joke. Now it's gone missing."

"Missing?" Aunt Folly looked up at the big, unfriendly woman.

"Perhaps it just walked out of the house," the minder said coldly.

Aunt Folly giggled. "But toys can't walk, can they?"

"They can jump, can't they?" Mrs Malevant said. "At least this one can." She didn't seem to be joking.

Bert opened his eyes and lifted his head.
One side of his face was patterned with blue squiggles.

Chapter Six

When the children got home from school, Sam and Miranda went straight to the kitchen. Izzy ran up to see Bert. She wasn't ready to face Mrs Malevant.

Bert's door had been unlocked, but he was fast asleep, his head on a sheet of messy paper.

"Bert!" Izzy shook his shoulder. "Wake up."

Bert opened his eyes and lifted his head. One side of his face was patterned with blue squiggles. Izzy couldn't stop herself from grinning. "You look like a sort of savage," she said. "What have you been doing?"

Bert didn't smile. "A hundred lines," he told Izzy. "I can't count to a hundred."

"I'll do them for you," Izzy offered. "She won't know it's my writing if I do them all."

"Thanks." Bert looked happier. "I'm sorry I got you into trouble."

"Not you." Izzy told him. "It was the panda."

"Was it?" Bert's eyes widened.

"'Fraid so." Izzy pulled up a chair and set to work. For a while Bert watched her hand fly across the page: he didn't want to stop her but there was something he had to ask. "Izzy, you said the panda did it. How?"

"I don't know," said Izzy. "But he can do that sort of thing. He told me."

"He talks?" Bert exclaimed.

"Ssh! Don't tell the others," Izzy said quickly.

Bert shook his head. "I promise I won't."

"You look hungry," said Izzy when she'd finished the last line of writing. "Come on. Let's go and see if tea's ready." She ran downstairs while Bert followed, holding the three finished pages of *I must not be greedy*.

Miranda and Sam were eating scones at the kitchen table.

"Scones!" cried Izzy. "I thought I could smell them."

Mrs Malevant snatched up the plate. "Not for you, Isabella, and not for Bert."

"But … but…" spluttered Izzy. "Sam and Miranda have had some. Why not us?"

Mrs Malevant ignored her. Miranda got up and left the room; she looked embarrassed. Sam whispered, "They're not that good."

"It's not fair," Izzy persisted. "A minder shouldn't have favourites. Mum never did."

Mrs Malevant said, "Don't argue."

Izzy opened her mouth to do just that when Miranda came tearing back, crying, "Someone's made a mess in my room and broken a china duck!"

"You again, Isabella?" said Mrs Malevant.

"I never," said Izzy.

"And what were you doing upstairs?" asked the minder.

Bert was about to tell, but Izzy said, "Ssh!"

"Ah, it *was* you all right," said Mrs Malevant. "I ought to…"

Izzy didn't wait to hear any more. She ran into the garden to get away from the minder's droning voice and the dreadful shadows in the unhappy house.

"It's not fair," she cried to the tall red building. "Nobody cares about Bert and me."

To make matters worse, the garden wasn't being cared for either. The flowers were wilting, the bird bath was empty and weeds

"It's not fair," Izzy cried to the tall red building.
"Nobody cares about Bert and me."

were poking their way through the path.

"I want someone to do something," Izzy told the house. "I want them to tell the minder to go."

But this couldn't be managed by anyone inside the house. Not yet.

Aunt Folly came tottering over the lawn. "Isabella, dear," she said. "What's all the fuss about?"

"I wish that, just for once, you'd be a proper auntie," said Izzy. "You're responsible for us, you know. You and Uncle Maurice. But you don't do anything."

"I can't think what you mean." Aunt Folly gave a toss of the head, allowing Izzy a better view of her neck. And all at once, Izzy realized what she was looking at.

"Those black beads on your necklace..." she said. "I always wondered where they came from."

Aunt Folly's hand flew to her throat. "I've had them ever since I was a girl," she mumbled. "I found them, a long time ago."

"They're eyes," said Izzy. "Panda's eyes!"

Aunt Folly gasped. "How did you…?" She turned quickly and flounced back into the house.

"Interesting," thought Izzy, calming down. "I wonder what really happened a long time ago?"

When she went back indoors she found that Mrs Malevant had calmed down as well. She agreed to let Izzy and Bert have their tea, which was dark brown stuff again, but luckily followed by pink ice-cream.

After tea Izzy trailed Miranda up to her room. "I didn't break your duck," Izzy said. "Really, I didn't."

"Then who did?" sniffed Miranda, re-positioning the two unbroken ducks. "I feel so sad when things get broken."

For the first time, Izzy actually felt sorry for Miranda. She seemed to need a tidy life much more than other people. Izzy had a good idea what might have happened, but could she convince Miranda? She decided to try. "It might have been the panda," she said.

"Don't be silly. Pandas can't walk. Not toy pandas anyway."

"I knew you wouldn't believe me." Izzy waltzed out.

She hardly believed it herself, so how could poor Miranda? Izzy decided to ask the panda what he'd been up to. But he wasn't in her room. She began to search the house and got Bert to join in.

"I don't want Mrs M to know what we're looking for," she told Bert, "or she might try and get rid of him again. I've got a feeling he broke Miranda's duck."

"How?" asked Bert.

"We'll never know. He can't move, you see, while he's being watched."

Bert was disappointed. "Perhaps if he didn't know he was being…"

"That wouldn't work," said Izzy. "He'd guess. Anyway it would be cheating."

Bert wanted to ask why but Izzy's expression stopped him, so they continued to search in silence, until they came to the sitting-room. Sam and Aunt Folly were watching a wildlife programme. Uncle Maurice was skulking behind his newspaper. The panda had slipped down the back of Aunt Folly's cushion: he wished he could see what was going on.

"We're looking for something," Izzy announced. "D'you mind if we move your cushions?"

63

"It takes me a long time to get comfy," Aunt Folly objected, "so I'd rather you didn't." She was still wearing the necklace and when Izzy stared at it, Aunt Folly quickly covered the black beads with her hand. "What are you looking for, dears?" she asked.

Izzy shot Bert a warning glance. "A book," she said.

"Sit down and watch this programme," said Sam. "It's very good."

So Izzy and Bert squeezed in beside Sam, but they'd hardly got comfortable when a voice from the doorway said, "Isabella and Bert, it's time for bed."

"But the sun's still shining," said Izzy in disbelief.

"It's been a long day," said the minder. "Bert, come here. You're still in disgrace."

Before Bert could move, Aunt Folly piped

64

up. "The children won't sleep. It's so light. And this is a very good programme, isn't it, Maurice?"

No help from that quarter. Uncle Maurice, hidden behind his paper, seemed to have been turned to stone.

Mrs Malevant shot Aunt Folly a dangerous look. "I have been hired to supervise these children," she growled. "Please don't interfere."

And that was that. Aunt Folly wilted into her chair. She couldn't look at Bert and Izzy, who obediently followed Mrs Malevant.

Squashed behind Aunt Folly's cushion, the panda felt helpless and sad. He heard people leaving the room. The television was turned off, and he waited for Aunt Folly to move, but it was a long time before she got to her feet. The room had become very dark and he could hardly see her.

"I'm sorry," she said in a trembly voice. "I'm truly sorry. Please believe me." Gently she eased Toby from his uncomfortable position and set him on a cushion. And then she stood in the dark for a long time, so long that the panda thought she must have crept away. But, all at once, he felt her cool hand on his ears, and something was slipped over his head. A string of beads.

When she had gone, the panda put up his paw and felt for the two black beads. "My eyes," he murmured. "My real eyes." Now he needed Izzy's help.

Toby slid off the chair and ran through the open door. He crossed the moonlit hall and mounted the stairs. When he reached the top landing he felt rather giddy and had to steady himself with a paw on the wall. Izzy's door was the last he came to. It was shut. Toby slumped to the floor.

The stairs creaked. Once. Twice. Some-one was still awake. Someone wearing soft-soled slippers was coming up to the top floor. A heavy person.

Creak! Creak! Creak! A night-light flickered in the distance. Now the heavy person was approaching Toby. He shrank back as the thin flame illumined the grim face above it.

"There you are," said Mrs Malevant. Her glittery stare bored right into him. "The jumping panda. Well, you won't get away from me this time."

Izzy bent to retrieve the panda, just as Mrs Malevant's hand came down a second time.

CHAPTER SEVEN

As Mrs Malevant's hand came down to grab him, the door behind Toby suddenly opened and he toppled back on to Izzy's feet.

"Mrs Malevant," said Izzy. "Is anything wrong?"

"Wrong? Of course not. I was just making sure all was well."

"Don't you have a torch?"

"Torches may be all the rage," said the minder. "I prefer a candle."

"Oh." Izzy bent to retrieve the panda, just as Mrs Malevant's hand came down a second time. Izzy got there first. Hugging the panda to her chest, she said, "Good night then, Mrs Malevant," and closed the door.

"Phew!" breathed Toby.

"Ssh!" Izzy crept back to bed. "She's still there, outside the door."

They waited in breathless silence until they heard the creak of Mrs Malevant's heavy feet receding, and then Izzy switched on her bedside light. "I want you to tell me the truth," she said. "Did you break Miranda's duck?"

"It was an accident," Toby confessed. "I only wanted to borrow her dressing-gown, but everything went wrong. Izzy, that horrible woman knows I can move. I gave myself away, just once, when—"

He was interrupted by a gasp from Izzy. "Panda, you've got Aunt Folly's necklace!"

"She gave it to me," the panda told her. "I think a long, long time ago, before I went into the attic, she took away my good eyes and gave me these instead. But now she's sorry."

Izzy lifted the necklace over the panda's head and held it under the light. The black beads were very beautiful. They had a deep, mysterious gleam. She touched them, reverently. "Did it hurt?" she asked in a hushed voice. "When you lost them?"

"It hurt my pride," the panda murmured. "But I'd already been abandoned."

"Oh, Panda!" Izzy hugged him. "I'll sew your eyes back on for you. And you'll never be abandoned again."

It was a wonderful thought, but Toby was still uneasy. "Just make sure that woman doesn't find me," he said.

"Promise," said Izzy. She tucked the necklace under her pillow and switched off the light.

*　　*　　*

Next morning Izzy felt ready for anything. It was Saturday. A whole day of freedom. She hid the panda at the bottom of her wardrobe and dashed downstairs.

"Late again, Isabella," Mrs Malevant greeted her.

The others were already eating their breakfasts. They all looked grim.

"It's Saturday," said Izzy. "I'm allowed to be late."

"Not in my house."

"This isn't *your* house," said Izzy bravely. "And soon you won't be here."

"Oh, ho. Won't I?" Mrs Malevant gave her a horrible smile. "That's where you're wrong."

Izzy sat down heavily. "What d'you mean?"

"I've had a phone call from your dad,"

said Mrs Malevant. "Your poor grandpa has had a nasty turn and so your mum and dad are staying on in Australia for a while, until he's quite better."

Izzy was thunderstruck. "How long?" she asked.

"Who knows?" Mrs Malevant's second smile was even worse than her first.

All at once Bert slumped forward over his cornflakes. His face was very white.

"What is it, Bert?" cried Izzy.

"I don't feel well," whispered Bert.

"Maybe we should phone the doctor," Sam suggested.

"Nonsense," said Mrs Malevant. "He ate too fast. He's greedy. Leave the table if you're going to be sick, boy."

Bert got up and, bent double, made for the door. Izzy was about to follow him when the minder shouted, "Sit down, or you'll regret

All at once Bert slumped forward over his cornflakes.
He face was very white.

it!" in such a loud voice that Izzy fell back into her chair with a bump.

After breakfast the others rushed up to see Bert. He was lying on his stomach with his face turned to the wall.

Sam and Izzy watched helplessly while Miranda fussed with Bert's pillow and put a blanket over him. "Oh dear! Oh dear!" she kept muttering.

"Something's got to be done," Sam said firmly. "I'm going to see Aunt Folly."

The girls trooped after him, down to the next floor and along the passage where a door stood ajar, revealing Aunt Folly at her dressing-table.

"Hullo, dears," said Aunt Folly. "You do look troubled."

"It's Bert." All three spoke together, and out came the story in short, sharp sentences until Sam's loud voice drowned out the others. "You've *got* to do something, Aunt Folly."

"Of course! Of course!" Aunt Folly ran into the passage, murmuring, "Poor Bert. I'll call the doctor right away."

"That won't be necessary, Miss Smith." Mrs Malevant stood at the top of the stairs.

"*I* think it's very necessary," said Aunt Folly. The children cuddled close to her, like chicks under a hen. "I'll look after things now, Mrs Malevant."

"Not a good idea," snapped the minder. "You're too old, Miss Smith. Things would go horribly wrong. You haven't got a clue what to do."

"H ... haven't I?" Aunt Folly's courage seemed to drain away. "No, I suppose I haven't," and to the children's horror, she crept back into her room, a faded, frail old lady.

"What have you done to our auntie?" cried Sam. "You're a bully, that's what you are, Mrs Malevant."

"Someone's got to take charge," said the minder. "You should thank your lucky stars I'm here," and she marched downstairs while Sam made a face behind her back.

"I'm going to ring the doctor, myself," whispered Miranda.

"Well done," breathed Izzy, surprised by this new, tender-hearted Miranda.

They crept downstairs and Miranda dialled the doctor's number while Sam stood guard outside the kitchen door.

Izzy leant close to Miranda, trying to hear the receptionist's voice.

"My brother's ill," Miranda explained. "Can the doctor come...? Yes, we've got a car. At least Mum and Dad have, but ... but ... oh!" She put down the receiver.

Aunt Folly looked so fragile, it was obvious she couldn't help anyone, even herself.

"Well?" said Sam and Izzy.

"We've got to get him to the surgery," Miranda said miserably.

"How? It's too far," said Sam.

They decided to see if Bert could manage a walk. He was lying with his knees drawn up to his chest and it didn't look as if he could go anywhere.

"I don't think I can move," he said.

Miranda brought Bert a glass of water and then all three marched back to see Aunt Folly, determined to make her help. But she looked so fragile, it was obvious she couldn't help anyone, even herself.

"What's happened, Aunt Folly?" asked Izzy. "Are you under a spell?"

"A sort of spell," said Aunt Folly. "I've always been afraid of bullies. I find it so hard to fight back. And you *could* say the house was spellbound too."

"The house?" chorused the three.

"It gets quite upset, you know," Aunt Folly said sadly, "when no one's happy. When the laughter dies. The stairs start groaning and the rooms grow dark and there's always a terrible draught in the hall. Haven't you noticed?"

The children nodded.

"Was it always like this?" asked Izzy.

"Always," said Aunt Folly. "I used to get bullied when I was little. I was such a small, quiet thing. And whenever I cried, the house would start fussing and rocking and groaning."

"Poor Aunt Folly," said Izzy, hugging her aunt.

"Didn't anyone help you?" asked Miranda. "You and the house?"

"Oh yes, Maurice helped," Aunt Folly smiled. "Maurice and Panda."

"Panda?" Izzy exclaimed.

Aunt Folly nodded. "That's right, the one that keeps turning up. I've forgotten his name. Máurice carried him everywhere. They seemed to belong together. He said the panda talked to him, and even moved by itself."

Miranda looked at Izzy.

"The panda made Maurice laugh, and somehow the laughter made me feel better, it cheered up the house and kept the bullies away. And then, one day, the boy next door told Maurice he was a sissy for carrying a panda around, and that was that." The twinkle in Aunt Folly's eye began to fade. "Maurice gave the panda to our mother and told her to pack him away."

Izzy was shocked. "Just like that, when they'd been such good friends?"

"He wanted to be grown up," Aunt Folly

explained. "I couldn't blame him." She hesitated, biting her lip. "Before the panda was put in the attic, I stole his eyes."

Miranda and Izzy gasped.

"I meant no harm," Aunt Folly went on in a quavery voice, "I just wanted to keep part of him with me, to give me courage. And I did sew a bit of cloth in their place. But when I saw him again, with those sad grey eyes, I felt so bad I gave him my necklace – to make up for what I did."

No one knew what to say to this, but at last Sam remarked, "It's strange that they both turned up on the very same day. Mrs Malevant and the panda."

"A problem and an answer," Aunt Folly said thoughtfully.

"D'you think that if Uncle Maurice and the panda were together again, they could make Mrs Malevant go away?" Izzy asked.

Aunt Folly sighed. "Your uncle doesn't recognize the poor thing. And he doesn't seem to care about anything. Doesn't want to. Perhaps, if he could remember what it was like to be young … if something could jog his memory…"

Izzy had an idea. "Can I borrow your sewing-kit, Aunt Folly?" she said.

Aunt Folly looked at Izzy. "Of course! I know what you want it for," she said, "and it just might work!"

When the house was dark and silent, Izzy took the panda out of his hiding place and laid him on her bed.

Chapter Eight

That night, when the house was dark and silent, Izzy took the panda out of his hiding place and laid him on her bed. Aunt Folly's sewing-kit was ready beside him: a basket of surgical instruments.

First she cut the two black beads from Aunt Folly's necklace and then she prepared for the difficult bit.

"This might hurt," she warned the panda. "I've got to snip out your cloth eyes before I put the black ones in. If the pain's too much, just raise a paw, like we do at the dentist, and I'll stop."

"I've never been to the dentist and I can't

raise a paw while you're looking," said the panda.

"Believe me, it can get nasty if you've got a sweet tooth," said Izzy, ignoring the bit about the paw.

"I haven't." He hardly noticed Izzy snipping and pulling the grey cloth away from his head, until she came to the last thread and everything went black.

"The light's gone out," gasped Toby.

"Patience," said Izzy. She placed a black bead on the panda's face and began to sew.

He tried to be patient, but it was so exciting. Slowly things swam into view. When the second eye went in, he could hardly keep still. The light was so bright, and the face above him so clear and sharp: a friendly face with pink cheeks and very bright brown eyes. Izzy as she really was.

"Thank you, Izzy," breathed the panda.

Izzy stood back to admire his new looks. What a difference they made, those gleaming black eyes.

"Handsome," she said, "very handsome." She tucked him under the covers and got into bed. Tomorrow, everything in the house would change.

Next morning, Izzy took a chance. A big chance. She sneaked the panda into the sitting-room and sat him in a chair right opposite Uncle Maurice's.

"You look great," she said. "Fantastic."

"I'm scared," Toby admitted. "Supposing that woman…"

"I won't let her," Izzy promised, and she ran into the kitchen to keep the minder occupied.

Mrs Malevant was eating black sausage and the room was filled with an awful smell.

Sam and Miranda kept blowing their noses. Bert was nowhere to be seen. *Could the panda make Bert better?* Izzy wondered.

Aunt Folly came in looking pale but determined. "I've been thinking," she said. "I can drive. I've still got a licence. I'll take Bert to the doctor."

Mrs Malevant gave a nasty snigger. "You," she said. "You can't see more than an inch in front of your face. You'd have an accident."

Aunt Folly went red, sat down and began to butter some toast.

Izzy listened for the front door. Where was Uncle Maurice? He always came in at nine o'clock on Sunday morning, with two newspapers under his arm. And he always went straight into the sitting-room, sat in his big armchair and read the papers right through till lunch-time. Izzy heard the front door slam. At last.

Uncle Maurice walked into the sitting-room, sat in his favourite chair and opened a newspaper. He began to read but found his attention wandering. He lowered the paper and saw that there was something in his sister's chair. It was looking at him.

Toby stared at Boy. At last he could really see him. Boy wasn't a ghost, but he had changed a great deal. Something strange had taken place in Boy's face. It was empty of the dreams that used to show so clearly. It was weary and forlorn and it hadn't laughed in ages.

"Boy," said the panda, "remember me?"

Boy frowned. He leaned forward and looked into Toby's shining eyes. Could he see himself reflected there?

"You *must* remember," the panda whispered.

* * *

In the kitchen Aunt Folly was helping herself to some trifle from the fridge.

"That was for lunch," said Mrs Malevant. "Kindly put it back."

This was more than Sam could take. "Stop bullying my auntie," he cried. "She can eat what she likes. You're making the whole house miserable."

"Too bad," said Mrs Malevant, smiling. "You're stuck with me, aren't you? I shall stay here as long as I … as I…"

Her voice was drowned by an amazing sound. A loud and very happy sound. It blew through the house like a merry breeze, brightening dark corners, brushing out shadows, rushing round unhappy rooms and cheering up the troubled stairs.

Uncle Maurice was laughing. They'd never heard him laugh before.

"Toby!" cried Uncle Maurice's happy voice. "It's you!"

Upstairs a door banged. There was a patter of feet on the stairs. "Uncle Maurice!" It was Bert, sounding very cheerful. "I think I feel better."

"Good! Good! Good!" said Uncle Maurice. "Let's go and tell the others."

The kitchen door burst open and Uncle Maurice strode in, clutching Bert by the hand.

"Look!" said Uncle Maurice, and he held up the panda. "It's Toby!" And then he noticed the minder. "Are you still here?" he barked.

A sound came from inside Mrs Malevant, as though she wanted to say something nasty but couldn't.

Uncle Maurice marched towards her. He looked quite splendid with his great crest of hair and his proud bony nose, like a white-haired wizard from the court of King Arthur.

"Go away!" he commanded. "You bully. And never darken our door again."

They watched the minder to see what she'd do. She looked so surprised it made Izzy giggle, and then Sam and Miranda joined in. Soon everyone in the kitchen was rocking with laughter and Izzy, glancing at Toby, knew he was laughing too.

How Mrs Malevant hated that sound! With her hands on her ears and her face pale and crumpled, she pushed past the happiness and ran out of the room – up the stairs for her coat and her suitcase. She couldn't run fast enough. Then the front door slammed and the minder was gone.

They never saw her again.

*   *   *

Mrs Malevant couldn't run fast enough.
The front door slammed and the minder was gone.

Later that day a crispy, spicy, toasty, sizzling smell wafted through the house. The children couldn't resist it. They went to the kitchen and found Uncle Maurice, in a bright blue apron, stirring a pan on the stove.

"This was my favourite dish when I was a boy," he said. "I hope you'll like it."

The children knew that they would.

Toby, sitting on a chair close to Boy, was struck by a sudden thought: *My name begins with T! The T that was missing from SMITH. We're a special family again!*

He noticed that Izzy was beaming at him. She had just had the very same thought.

THE

END